AMY WU
and the
WARM
WELCOME

Japanese

ようこそ

Vietnamese

Chào
mừng!

Italian

Benvenuto!

Spanish

¡Bienvenido!

Malay and Indonesian

Selamat
datang!

Ways to say "Welcome" around the world.

Turkish
Hoşgeldiniz!

Farsi
خوش آمدید

Korean
안녕하세요!

Hindi
स्वागत!

For every child who has been the new kid in a new land—K. Z.

For Milo and Rox—C. C.

SIMON & SCHUSTER BOOKS FOR YOUNG READERS • An imprint of Simon & Schuster Children's Publishing Division • 1230 Avenue of the Americas, New York, New York 10020 • Text © 2022 by Kat Zhang • Illustration © 2022 by Charlene Chua • Book design by Laura Lyn DiSiena © 2022 by Simon & Schuster, Inc. • All rights reserved, including the right of reproduction in whole or in part in any form. • SIMON & SCHUSTER BOOKS FOR YOUNG READERS and related marks are trademarks of Simon & Schuster, Inc. • For information about special discounts for bulk purchases, please contact Simon & Schuster Special Sales at 1-866-506-1949 or business@simonandschuster.com. • The Simon & Schuster Speakers Bureau can bring authors to your live event. For more information or to book an event contact the Simon & Schuster Speakers Bureau at 1-866-248-3049 or visit our website at www.simonspeakers.com. • The text of this book was set in Andes Rounded. • The illustrations for this book were rendered digitally. • Manufactured in China • 0122 SCP • First Edition • 10 9 8 7 6 5 4 3 2 1 • Library of Congress Cataloging-in-Publication Data • Names: Zhang, Kat, 1991– author. | Chua, Charlene, illustrator. • Title: Amy Wu and the warm welcome / Kat Zhang ; illustrated by Charlene Chua. • Description: First edition. | New York : Simon & Schuster Books for Young Readers, [2022] | Audience: Ages 4–8. | Audience: Grades K–1. | Summary: Amy Wu would love to welcome the new student in her class, but Lin has just come from China and does not speak much English, so with the help of her family Amy tries to work out a way to bridge the language gap. • Identifiers: LCCN 2021014126 (print) | LCCN 2021014127 (ebook) | ISBN 9781534497351 (hardcover) | ISBN 9781534497368 (ebook) • Subjects: LCSH: Chinese Americans—Juvenile fiction. | Immigrants—Juvenile fiction. | Friendship—Juvenile fiction. | Schools—Juvenile fiction. | CYAC: Immigrants—Fiction. | Friendship—Fiction. | Schools—Fiction. | Chinese Americans—Fiction. • Classification: LCC PZ7.Z454 Ap 2022 (print) | LCC PZ7.Z454 (ebook) | DDC [E]—dc23 • LC record available at https://lccn.loc.gov/2021014126 • LC ebook record available at https://lccn.loc.gov/2021014127

AMY WU
and the
WARM
WELCOME

By **KAT ZHANG** ✦ Illustrated by **CHARLENE CHUA**

SIMON & SCHUSTER BOOKS FOR YOUNG READERS
New York London Toronto Sydney New Delhi

When Amy arrives at school, Ms. Mary has a wonderful surprise . . . **a new student!**

"This is Lin," says Ms. Mary. "He moved here from China. Can everyone give him a **big, warm welcome**?"

"Welcome, Lin!"
says Amy's class.

Lin grins and opens his mouth.

Then he shuts it again.

His cheeks glow red.

For lunch Lin eats dumplings and tangerines.

"I'm having a dumpling party tonight!" Amy says.

"Did you make those?"

Lin smiles but doesn't reply.

During playtime Amy invites Lin aboard her pirate ship.

He puts on a hat but doesn't sing **"YO-HO!"**

During show-and-tell Amy picks Lin to share his favorite sport. He holds up a soccer ball but doesn't say a word.

"Wow, a new classmate!" says Mom after school. "Did you make him feel welcome?"

"I **tried**," says Amy. "But I don't know if I did."

Just then, Lin's dad arrives with Lin's little sister.

Lin's face **lights up**.

He giggles and chatters in Chinese.

His sister giggles and chatters in Chinese.

This is a whole new Lin!

Amy ponders the two Lins as she and her mom arrive at the store. She ponders while they buy dumpling skins. She ponders while they choose dumpling fillings.

ginger

bok choy

garlic

scallions

cabbage

mushrooms

Amy's mom looks in their cart. "That's enough for our guests, don't you think?"

Amy's pondering becomes a **brilliant plan**.

"Will it be enough for a few more?" she asks.

At home Amy's grandma helps her roll out a long sheet of paper. Amy chooses her favorite markers.

Then Grandma writes the message while Amy says it aloud.

She already knows the characters:

"Huan" starts out soft like the hoot of an owl.

"Ying" flies from her tongue like the ring of a bell.

And "ni" sounds a lot like "knee."

All together, it means **"welcome."**
And **"welcome"** is exactly what
Amy wants to say.

Amy waits with her banner as the guests arrive.

First come her parents' friends from work.

Then come Amy's friends from school.

And finally, there is **Lin**!

Amy's hands tighten on her banner.

She grins and opens her mouth.

Then she shuts it again.

Her cheeks glow red.

Everyone is watching.

But the words stick in Amy's throat.

She thinks the characters in her mind:

"**Huan**" starts out soft like the hoot of an owl.

"**Ying**" flies from her tongue like the ring of a bell.

And "**ni**" sounds a lot like "knee."

欢

迎

你

But she can't say them, no matter how hard she tries.

A finger taps on her shoulder. Lin points to the table where the grown-ups are making dumplings.

He doesn't say anything,
but Amy understands.

Lin makes a dumpling shaped like a little **boat**.

Amy makes a dumpling shaped like a little **purse**.

Boat, boat, boat.

Purse, purse, purse.

Together, their dumplings tumble into the pot.

The boats float beside the purses. The purses float beside the boats.

Everyone eats dumplings until they can't eat another bite.

It's time for Lin to go home.

Amy sees her banner.

She takes a deep breath.

"Huan" starts out soft like the hoot of an owl.

"Ying" flies from her tongue like the ring of a bell.

欢 迎 你

And **"ni"** sounds a lot like "knee."

Amy's family laughs.
"Silly goose," they say. "'Welcome'
is for the beginning of a party,
not the end."

But Amy knows better.

It's never too late for a welcome.

MAKE A WELCOME BANNER

In this book, Amy welcomes Lin to her class. How would you welcome someone to your school or hometown? A banner is a great way to start! It shows your excitement and can tell them about their new school or home.

YOU WILL NEED:

Craft paper, poster board, or construction paper

Art supplies for decorating

Lots of heart and imagination!

IDEAS TO INCLUDE ON A BANNER WELCOMING A NEW STUDENT TO YOUR SCHOOL:

1. The best reading nook

2. The most exciting school event of the year

3. The tastiest food served by the cafeteria

4. A good person to ask for help

IDEAS TO INCLUDE ON A BANNER WELCOMING A NEW FRIEND TO YOUR HOMETOWN:

1. The best place to go swimming

2. Where to have a fun picnic

3. Your favorite way to spend a weekend

4. Your favorite restaurant

Feel free to add your own ideas!
What are things you'd like to know about a new school or neighborhood?

When I was growing up, I was usually the only child in my class who spoke both English and Mandarin. This meant teachers sometimes asked me to translate for Mandarin-speaking kids who joined our school and were not yet fluent in English. This experience from my childhood was the inspiration for *Amy Wu and the Warm Welcome*. It was important to me to include a scene where Lin spoke in Chinese with his family. A lesson I've learned is that people can seem so different when you communicate with them in a way that's familiar and comfortable to them!

—K. Z.